The Books About Samantha

❧

Meet Samantha · An American Girl

Samantha becomes good friends with Nellie, a servant girl, and together they plan a secret midnight adventure.

❧

Samantha Learns a Lesson · A School Story

Samantha becomes Nellie's teacher, but Nellie has some very important lessons to teach Samantha, too.

❧

Samantha's Surprise · A Christmas Story

Uncle Gard's friend Cornelia is ruining Samantha's Christmas. But Christmas morning brings surprises!

❧

Happy Birthday, Samantha! · A Springtime Story

When Eddie Ryland spoils Samantha's birthday party, Cornelia's twin sisters know just what to do.

❧

Samantha Saves the Day · A Summer Story

Samantha enjoys a peaceful summer at Piney Point, until a terrible storm strands her on Teardrop Island!

❧

Changes for Samantha · A Winter Story

When Samantha finds out that her friend Nellie is living in an orphanage, she must think of a way to help her escape.

SAMANTHA'S SURPRISE
A CHRISTMAS STORY

BY MAXINE ROSE SCHUR

ILLUSTRATIONS NANCY NILES, R. GRACE

VIGNETTES EILEEN POTTS DAWSON

PLEASANT COMPANY

Published by Pleasant Company Publications Incorporated
© Copyright 1986 by Pleasant Company Incorporated
All rights reserved. No part of this book may be used or reproduced in
any manner whatsoever without written permission except in the case of
brief quotations embodied in critical articles and reviews.
For information, address: Book Editor,
Pleasant Company Publications Incorporated,
8400 Fairway Place, P.O. Box 620998,
Middleton, WI 53562.

First Edition.
Printed in the United States of America.
95 96 97 98 RND 30 29 28 27 26

The American Girls Collection® is a registered trademark of
Pleasant Company Incorporated.

PICTURE CREDITS
The following individuals and organizations have generously given
permission to reprint illustrations contained in "Looking Back":
pp. 62-63—Clarence P. Hornung, *Handbook of Early Advertising Art*
(Dover Publications, Inc., New York, 1947); State Historical Society of
Wisconsin; Bergmann Collection, State Historical Society of Wisconsin; pp.
64-65—Gesell Collection, State Historical Society of Wisconsin; Krueger
Collection, State Historical Society of Wisconsin; pp. 66-67—Smith
Collection, State Historical Society of Wisconsin; State Historical Society
of Wisconsin.

Edited by Jeanne Thieme
Designed by Myland McRevey

Library of Congress Cataloging-in-Publication Data

Schur, Maxine Rose
Samantha's surprise: a Christmas story

(The American girls collection)
Summary: The two weeks before Christmas are filled with activity as Samantha
finishes her homemade presents and makes preparations for
visiting relatives.
[1. Christmas–Fiction]
I. Niles, Nancy, ill.   II. Grace, Robert, ill.   III. Title.   IV. Series.
PZ7.S3964Sam 1986   [Fic]   86-60625
ISBN 0-937295-86-8
ISBN 0-937295-22-1 (pbk.)

TO LILIANA, CECILIA,
AND SUSANA

TABLE OF CONTENTS

SAMANTHA'S FAMILY

GRANDMARY
*Samantha's
grandmother, who
wants her
to be a young lady.*

SAMANTHA
*A nine-year-old
orphan who lives
with her wealthy
grandmother.*

NELLIE
*Samantha's friend
who works
as a maid.*

UNCLE GARD
*Samantha's
favorite uncle, who
calls her Sam.*

CORNELIA
*An old-fashioned
beauty who has
new-fangled ideas.*

HAWKINS
*Grandmary's butler
and driver, who
is Samantha's friend.*

MRS. HAWKINS
*Grandmary's cook,
who always has
a treat for
Samantha.*

JESSIE
*Grandmary's
seamstress, who
"patches
Samantha up."*

ELSA
*The maid, who
is usually grumpy.*

IDA DEAN
*Samantha's friend,
who is planning
the best Christmas
party ever.*

CHRISTMAS
WISHES

"Wait, Samantha! I want to give you this." Samantha's friend Ida pressed a red envelope into her hand.

Samantha pulled off her mittens, tore open the flap, and drew out a card shaped like a Christmas stocking and edged with paper lace. It said:

*Miss Ida Dean requests
the pleasure of your company
at a Christmas Party
to be held at
six o'clock in the evening
Thursday, December 22
R.S.V.P.*

"Ooh, Ida," Samantha squealed. Her breath made little clouds in the chilly December air.

"I hope you can come," Ida said. "My brother is going to do magic tricks, and we'll play ladies' ring and charades!"

"Ida, it sounds wonderful!" Samantha said. "I think this is going to be the best Christmas ever!"

"Me, too," Ida agreed. "Especially if I get a new pair of ice skates. But do you know what I really want?"

"A dollhouse?" Samantha guessed.

"No."

"A sled?"

"No."

STEREOSCOPE

"A stereoscope?"

"No. A dog," Ida said. "A real cocker spaniel puppy!"

"Puppies are so cute! Do you think you'll get one?" Samantha asked.

"I don't know. I've asked and asked, though," Ida replied. "What are you hoping for?"

Samantha sighed. "What I really want is the doll I saw at Schofield's Toy Store," she said. "I want that doll more than anything in the world!"

"What's she like?" Ida wondered.

"She's beautiful," Samantha replied. "She's dressed all in pink, even her shoes, and in her hand there's a tiny little—"

"Let's go look!" Ida interrupted.

The two girls raced down the street. As they ran, snowflakes swirled around them, clinging to their knitted mittens, resting in their hair, and brushing their cheeks like small, quick kisses.

At Schofield's Toy Store, the girls pressed their noses to the cold glass window. "There she is!" Samantha breathed. She pointed to a group of dolls that seemed to be dancing. They twirled around a taller doll who wore a lacy pink dress, pink pantalets, and pink slippers. The doll held a tiny wooden soldier that looked just like the Nutcracker in the ballet.

"I love that Nutcracker doll," Samantha said.

"Well, do you think your grandmother will give it to you?" Ida asked.

"No . . ." Samantha answered slowly, looking down at her wet black boots. "I don't think so. I haven't asked her."

"I love that Nutcracker doll,"
Samantha said.

"You haven't *asked?*" Ida was puzzled. "Why not?"

"I just can't."

"What do you mean you *can't?*" Ida's voice rose. "Why can't you?"

"Because of Lydia," Samantha replied, remembering the beautiful doll that had been in Schofield's window last summer. Samantha had wanted that doll so much that Grandmary had bought it for her.

"You mean because you gave Lydia away?" Ida asked.

Samantha nodded.

"I would never, ever give a doll away. Especially a doll my grandmother had given to me!" Ida declared.

"But I gave Lydia to my friend Nellie. She had never owned a doll in her life. Not ever!"

"Oh." Ida paused. Then she added, "Well, now *you* don't have a doll. So why don't you ask your grandmother for this one?"

Samantha took one last look at the doll in the window, then shook her head. "I just don't think Grandmary would buy me another doll so soon.

expecting this gingerbread house to be?"

"About two feet across and two feet high."

"Two feet high! And you're sure this isn't a gingerbread train station?" Mrs. Hawkins teased.

"It *is* rather big," Samantha admitted, "but it's got to hold up a lot of things. We'll use taffy sticks for pillars and caramel squares for the doors. Cinnamon drops make the best chimney bricks, and for the drawbridge we can use licorice ropes!"

"My!" Mrs. Hawkins said. "It certainly sounds fancy."

"But we can do it—I know we can. Don't you think so, Mrs. Hawkins?" Samantha asked.

Mrs. Hawkins looked over the drawing again. "Yes, Samantha, I do believe that with a lot of ingredients, and quite a bit of time, and just a pinch of luck, we can make this house."

"Oh, I knew you'd say yes, Mrs. Hawkins. Thank you so much!" Samantha cried, jumping up and giving her a hug. "Let's do it Saturday!"

8

CHAPTER
TWO
—

PRESENTS AND A
PARTY DRESS

 Samantha went up to her bedroom, closed the door, and turned the big brass key to lock it. Then she pulled her chair into the closet and climbed up on it. From the top of the chair she could just reach the big pink hatbox on the highest shelf. She brought it down and set it carefully on her bed.

The hatbox was Samantha's Christmas box. It held all the presents she was making. She unpacked them now, one by one.

First she lifted out the satin pincushion she'd made for Jessie, the seamstress. It was shaped like a strawberry and stuffed with a cup of sawdust from the butcher shop.

Next Samantha took out a book about a lost dog. It was for Nathaniel, Jessie's baby. Samantha had written it herself and stitched it together with red yarn.

Grandmary's gift was underneath the book. It was a heart made from lace and stuffed with dried rose petals. Samantha sniffed it. She knew Grandmary would put it with her handkerchiefs to make them smell pretty.

Mrs. Hawkins' gift was a chain to attach to her glasses so she'd never lose them again. And for Nellie, Samantha had made a blue velvet cape for Lydia to wear. Samantha held the cape and thought about how beautiful Lydia would look in it.

At last Samantha reached her favorite gift of all. It was for Uncle Gard. Uncle Gard's present wasn't finished yet, but already it was more beautiful than anything Samantha had ever made. It was a box—a small box, just the right size for cuff links. Samantha had decorated it with pictures of animals, leaves, berries, fruits, and flowers from her collection of paper scraps. She had carefully cut out each piece of scrap. Then she'd glued them, one by one, to the sides of the box.

PIECES OF SCRAP

Now only the lid was left to be decorated. Samantha sat on the floor with her pot of glue and her collection of scraps spread around her. Very, very carefully she brushed the back of a purple pansy with glue and held it firmly on to the box. After the glue had dried she picked up one last picture—her favorite one. It was a heart with the words "with love" written on it. Carefully, Samantha placed it in the very center of the lid. It was perfect. She *knew* Uncle Gard would like this present best of any he would get on Christmas morning.

Just then someone knocked at her door.

"Miss Samantha."

"Just a minute, Jessie!" Samantha called. Quickly, she stuffed her presents back into the hatbox and pushed it under her bed.

"Open the door, child!"

Samantha hid her scrap collection next to the hatbox, scooted the chair out of her closet, and hurried to unlock her bedroom door.

"Come along, now. I've finished your Christmas dress. We just need to hem it," the

11

seamstress said. Samantha followed her upstairs into the little sewing room. She could hardly wait to see the new party dress Jessie had made.

"Where is it?" Samantha asked, looking around the room.

"Oh, you'll see it in good time," Jessie said, smiling slyly. "Now, take off that dress, close your eyes, and raise your arms."

Samantha did as she was told and felt something crisp and cool slide over her head.

"Heavens!" Jessie gasped.

"What's the matter?" Samantha asked, keeping her eyes closed.

"Why, you've grown two inches since I measured you. Miss Samantha, you shoot up faster than smoke in a chimney!"

"May I open my eyes now, Jessie?"

"Not just yet. First let me fix the hem. That'll make a big difference."

Samantha waited patiently with her eyes still closed. "Jessie?"

"Mmmmm?" Jessie's mouth was full of pins.

"Ida Dean is having a Christmas party in two weeks. Do you think I can wear this dress?"

Jessie pulled the last pins out of her mouth. "I don't know, child. You'll have to ask your grandmother."

"Jessie . . . ?" Samantha started up again.

"Yes, Miss Samantha?"

"I just love Christmas. I love everything about it. Even getting ready for Christmas is fun."

"I'm sure it is," Jessie laughed.

"I've made all the decorations for the house already," Samantha added. "I've got paper snowflakes and cotton snowmen and things for the tree. And on Saturday morning, Nellie is coming over to help me make pine cone wreaths."

"Did you make the angels out of that blue silk I gave you?" Jessie asked.

"I made ten of them, just the way you showed me!"

"You *have* been working hard!" Jessie said.

"Now can I see myself, Jessie?" Samantha asked eagerly.

"Yes, it's all done."

Samantha opened her eyes and faced the long mirror. Slowly, she turned herself around. The red taffeta dress shimmered and made ever-so-soft

"Playing dress up at this hour!"
Elsa snipped.

swishing sounds as Samantha moved. It was the color of ripe cranberries. A snowy white lace collar circled the neck, and a crisp white sash wrapped her hips and tied in a bow in front.

"Jessie, this is the most gorgeous dress in the whole world," Samantha pronounced solemnly.

"I agree with you there, Miss Samantha! It's a dress fine enough for a princess, if I do say so myself!"

Samantha heard someone sniff. Elsa, the maid, was standing at the door scowling. "Playing dress up at this hour!" she snipped. "It's all very well to fuss with them frills, but not at teatime. Your grandmother told me to fetch you, and here you are not even properly dressed!"

"Now, Elsa. Miss Samantha will be right down," Jessie answered.

"Fussing with frills at teatime!" Elsa muttered to herself as she turned. Her shoes scolded "tsk tsk tsk" as she walked down the hall.

Jessie helped Samantha out of the new dress and back into her regular clothes. Samantha straightened her stockings and raced downstairs.

"Grandmary, Grandmary!" she burst out.

She remembered to make a curtsy. "I have the most exciting news!"

"How delightful," replied her silver-haired grandmother as she lifted the teapot. "Come, let's have our tea."

Just as Samantha was sure she couldn't wait a moment longer, her grandmother asked, "And what is your news, Samantha?"

"My friend Ida Dean is having a Christmas party. It's a week from Thursday, and it's at night! Her brother will do magic tricks and we're going to play games, and it will be the most wonderful party of all. May I go? And may I wear my new Christmas dress?"

Grandmary took a sip of tea. "Samantha dear, you really must learn to ask only *one* question at a time. *Two* questions at once are quite . . . unbalancing. Now, as to the first question—of course you may go, my dear. And as to the second question—yes, you may wear your new dress. You grow so fast, you might as well get all the wear you can out of it."

"Thank you, Grandmary," Samantha said happily. "I'll have the best time."

"And now I have a surprise for you," Grandmary announced.

There was a long pause as Grandmary buttered a biscuit. She was not one to hurry surprises. Finally she said, "As you know, Samantha, your Uncle Gardner will spend Christmas with us as he always has. But this year he is not coming alone. He is bringing Miss Cornelia Pitt with him. She will celebrate the holidays here in Mount Bedford and stay on until the New Year."

Miss Cornelia Pitt? Grandmary meant Cornelia! Samantha thought of Uncle Gard's dark-haired friend who lived in New York. Cornelia was beautiful and so elegant. Her clothes were the latest style, and she always smelled of violets.

"Remember, Samantha," Grandmary continued, "Cornelia is a special friend of your uncle's. We must make her feel welcome."

"Oh, I'll welcome her," Samantha said. "And I'll make this the best Christmas *she's* ever had, too. That will be easy. I've already made all the decorations and planned the gingerbread house."

"That's very good of you, Samantha,"

Grandmary said. "But perhaps you have done enough already. Everyone in the house will be very busy now, and it may be best if you just stay out of the way."

Samantha wondered why grownups always thought the most helpful thing she could do was nothing at all. Didn't they understand what still had to be done? Someone had to string cranberries and hang snowflakes on the windows. Someone had to pick out just the right candy for the gingerbread house. Someone had to help Uncle Gard find a perfect Christmas tree. Samantha could do all those things. And now that Cornelia was coming, she had more to do. She would have to get one more present—something very nice and very elegant for Cornelia. But what? What??

"It's so *hard* to figure out gifts!" Samantha found herself saying aloud.

"What is that you said, dear?" Grandmary asked.

"I was just thinking, Grandmary, how hard it is to know what somebody might want for Christmas. I mean, most of the time you just have to guess!"

Grandmary smiled. "You're entirely correct,

Samantha. Of course, sometimes a person might let you know what may be appropriate."

"Yes, Grandmary," Samantha said, remembering her own secret wish for Christmas. She thought of what Ida had said, and the words floated back to her. *You should ask her anyway,* they whispered. *The worst she can say is no.*

"Grandmary," Samantha said, clearing her throat.

"Yes, Samantha?" her grandmother answered, not looking up as she poured more tea.

"Grandmary, I wanted to ask if . . . if . . ."

"Yes?" Now Grandmary seemed to stare right through Samantha.

"Grandmary, I just wanted to ask you if . . . well . . ."

"Samantha dear, speak up. I can hardly hear you when you mumble!"

"Grandmary, I wanted to tell you that . . ."

"Come to the point, Samantha."

". . . that I think it's going to snow through the weekend!" Samantha blurted out, red-faced and shy.

"Yes, dear, I quite agree with you."

It was no use. Samantha knew she couldn't ask Grandmary for the doll. She didn't have the courage.

CHAPTER
THREE

DECORATIONS AND DISAPPOINTMENTS

On Saturday morning, when their pine cone wreaths were made, Samantha showed Nellie some of the presents in her pink hatbox. She saved Uncle Gard's box until last. "And this is the best present of all," she said proudly as she handed it to Nellie.

"Oh, it really is," Nellie agreed. "I know your uncle will like it."

"He'll *love* it," Samantha insisted. "He'll know it's the nicest thing I've ever made for anyone."

"What are you giving your grandmother?" Nellie asked.

Samantha showed her the sweet-smelling sachet she had made. "Grandmary says home-

made gifts are the best ones because you give of
yourself when you make them. But I'll have to buy
Cornelia's present. There's not enough time to make
something really special for her," Samantha said. "I
wish I knew what to get."

"What about bath salts?" Nellie suggested.
"Mrs. Van Sicklen has some in a tall bottle with a
fancy glass top."

"Yes, bath salts are nice," Samantha agreed.
Then she shook her head. "But I don't think bath
salts are nice enough for Cornelia."

"How about hankies?" Nellie asked.

"Well, maybe if they had lace edges,"
Samantha said hopefully. Then she thought of
Cornelia riding in Uncle Gard's automobile, and
even hankies with lace edges seemed like a dull
sort of present. "No, Nellie, I need to think of

something *really* special."

"Perfume?" Nellie suggested.

"That would be special enough, but
I don't think I have enough money for
perfume." Samantha sighed. "Well, I
can go talk to Jessie later. Maybe she'll know what I
should get for Cornelia."

"I'm giving Mrs. Van Sicklen my biggest pine cone wreath," Nellie said. She looked proudly at the wreaths she'd lined up on the floor of Samantha's room. "Do you think she'll like it?"

"Of course she will," Samantha assured her friend. "Everyone loves Christmas decorations." She reached under her bed, pulled out a cardboard box with DECORATIONS written on all four sides, and took out the cotton snowmen, silk angels, and paper snowflakes she'd been making since Thanksgiving. "Look what I'm putting up this afternoon," she said.

"Samantha, your house is going to look like a fairyland," Nellie exclaimed.

"Especially with these snowflakes," Samantha agreed.

Later that afternoon, after Nellie had gone home, Samantha lugged her decoration box down the long winding staircase. *I'll trim the banister first,*

she thought. At the bottom of the stairs she unpacked a long string of cranberries. She was about to wind it around the polished railing when a strange voice stopped her.

"Excuse me, young lady," said a tall red-haired man. He wore a navy blue uniform almost like a soldier's. The words *Farrola Florist* were on the right pocket.

The man set down a large box that held spicy-scented garlands with enormous red bows. He drew a garland out slowly, handling it as delicately as if it were a snake. "Now if you would just step out of the way, miss," he continued as he began to wrap the garland gracefully around the banister.

 "I have some decorations, too," Samantha told the man. "I have a cranberry garland. Well, I guess you'd call it a string of cranberries. It would look quite nice together with—"

"Please, miss," the red-haired man sighed, "if you could just stand back and try not to disturb the garland. It's a bit fragile."

Samantha stepped back and found herself standing on Hawkins' toes.

"Oh, Hawkins, I'm so sorry," she said.

"That's quite all right, Miss Samantha. Now if you'll excuse me. . . ."

Hawkins was carrying another box marked *Farrola Florist* into the parlor. Two more large boxes were already on the rug.

"What's in all these boxes?" asked Samantha.

"Holiday adornments," he said. "Christmas decorations." Samantha saw holly and laurel wreaths and bouquets of Christmas roses—red ones, of course. She counted four ropes of ivy, eight hoops of mistletoe, and two miniature trees. One

was trimmed with little crab apples and one was
full of tiny oranges. "Your grandmother wishes the
house to be in full Yuletide splendor for Miss
Cornelia's visit," Hawkins explained. He turned to
drape an ivy rope across the fireplace mantle.

Samantha could not believe what she was
seeing. "But Hawkins, I've already *made*
decorations, lots of them, enough for the whole
house!"

Hawkins was struggling so hard with the ivy
that he didn't seem to hear.

Samantha picked up her box of decorations and
walked into the dining room. No one was around,

 so she took out her fuzzy snowmen
first. She hung six of them from the
wall lamps, using green ribbon. Two
more were soon propped up beside the
huge meat platter on the china cabinet. Four
snowmen stood together around a pile of pine
cones in the center of the table.

Using the tiniest drops of glue, Samantha stuck
paper snowflakes to the dining room windows. She
took down a small oil painting and in its place
hung her largest pine cone wreath. The cranberry

garland went across the dining room curtains.

When Samantha had finished, she sat down to admire her work. The whole room was like a tiny indoor forest filled with pine cones and red berries. Cotton snowmen peeked out from the dark furniture as if they were hiding behind tall trees. Paper snowflakes seemed to float on the windows. *It's beautiful,* Samantha thought. *It's like a winter wonderland—and I did it all by myself.*

Someone gasped. "Sakes alive! What is this nonsense?"

It was Elsa.

The maid went straight to the windows and began tearing off Samantha's snowflakes. "It's not as if a body didn't have enough to do, what with the washing and dusting and polishing," Elsa muttered. "And now having to put up with all this holiday hoopla. Whatever made the child set all them dustcatchers around?"

Samantha jumped out of her chair. "They're not dustcatchers! They're snowflakes and cranberry garlands and snowmen and . . . and . . . and I made them!"

Elsa was speechless for a moment. Then she

*"They're not dustcatchers! They're snowflakes
and I made them!" Samantha said.*

28

said firmly, "Mr. Hawkins and a young florist gentleman are decorating the house just as your grandmother wished—fine and fancy for Miss Cornelia's visit. So it's no use trying to tell me about your snowmice!"

"Snow*men*," Samantha sniffed, scooping up the decorations that Elsa had piled on the floor.

"Whatever," Elsa said. "Run along now. I've got the devil's own work dusting this chandelier. Miss Cornelia will be here for Christmas dinner, and it's got to sparkle."

"You'd think it was Cornelia Day, not Christmas Day," Samantha grumbled, almost loud enough for Elsa to hear. She went to the kitchen. Maybe a visit with Mrs. Hawkins would cheer her up.

The kitchen was perfumed with delicious smells. Two mince pies and a pound cake had just come out of the oven. There were homemade peppermint drops cooling on the table. At the sink, Mrs. Hawkins was pouring quince jam into glass jars. Her face was as red as the cranberry sauce that bubbled on the stove.

Samantha sat down at the table and popped one of the peppermint drops into her mouth. "You know, Mrs. Hawkins," she said, "I just thought of a good idea."

There was no answer.

"Mrs. Hawkins?"

"Yes, dear," Mrs. Hawkins replied, not looking up from her jam.

"I said that I just thought of something."

"Hmmm, what's that?"

"Well, we could cover the walls of the gingerbread house with peppermint drops and it would look like a magic candy house—like the candy house in *Hansel and Gretel.*"

"Samantha," Mrs. Hawkins said with a sigh, "I know you'll be disappointed, but I don't see that we can make a gingerbread house after all. With your Uncle Gard's friend coming and your grandmother wanting everything so special for her, there's a tremendous lot of cooking to be done. There's just no time for a gingerbread house this year."

"Not *any* gingerbread house?" Samantha asked with disbelief. "Not even a little one?"

"Not even a little one, Samantha. Truly I'm

sorry, but I think you're old enough to understand."

"Yes, I understand," said Samantha sadly. "I really do, Mrs. Hawkins." She left the kitchen mumbling, "I understand that if Cornelia weren't coming, everything would be fine."

She picked up her box of decorations and hauled it up the stairway. The corner of the box bumped the garland on the banister and knocked a bow crooked. Samantha didn't straighten it.

In her room, Samantha unpacked her decorations again. *I'll put them up here,* she said to herself. *If everyone else thinks snowflakes are a bother, then they can stay out of my room.* She noticed that two of her best snowflakes had been ruined and decided to make new ones. She went to her desk to hunt for a pair of scissors.

Why is everyone making such a fuss over Cornelia? Samantha asked herself as she folded a piece of tissue paper. *There's nothing special about her. Nothing special at all. I don't know why I even bothered to worry about her present. I'll just give her hankies for Christmas. Plain, boring, lie-in-the-box hankies!*

There was a knock at Samantha's door. She

opened it to find Grandmary standing there.

"Samantha dear, your Uncle Gardner has just telephoned to say that he and Cornelia will arrive late Thursday afternoon. We must welcome Cornelia properly, so I am afraid that going to a party that evening is out of the question. You will need to send Ida Dean your regrets."

"Oh, Grandmary, no!" Samantha cried.

Grandmary's face said it was useless to argue, and just to be sure she added, "It is the polite thing to do, Samantha." She said it kindly, but Samantha knew she didn't expect to say it again.

Stupid Cornelia is ruining Christmas, Samantha thought. *She's ruining it for everybody, but mostly she's ruining it for me. I'm not allowed to decorate my house and I can't make a gingerbread house, either. Now I can't go to Ida's party, so I won't be able to play charades or see magic tricks or wear my beautiful new dress!*

"I hate Cornelia!" Samantha said when she was sure Grandmary couldn't hear her. Slowly, hot tears began to roll down her cheeks.

"I'm glad I don't have enough money to buy her perfume. I won't buy her handkerchiefs, either.

I wouldn't give Cornelia bath salts in a paper bag. In fact, I won't give her anything at all for Christmas." The tears came faster, and Samantha began to sob.

—

SOMEONE
VERY SPECIAL

"Your house looks especially lovely with all the Christmas decorations," Cornelia said. Sunlight poured through the parlor windows and danced in her wavy dark hair.

"Thank you," Grandmary answered. "We did want things to be festive for you."

Samantha didn't say anything. She didn't even look at Cornelia.

"I hope the trip down wasn't too tiring for you," said Grandmary as she passed a plate of tiny tea sandwiches.

"Oh, no," Cornelia replied. "I do love motor cars, and Gard—I mean Gardner—is such a good driver."

Grandmary smiled. "You are certainly brave, my dear, to ride in those new machines."

"I love travel of any kind," Cornelia responded, her brown eyes sparkling. "When the new flying machines begin to carry passengers, I plan to ride in one of them, too."

So do I! Samantha thought. *I'd love to see Mount Bedford the way a bird sees it!*

Grandmary raised her eyebrows. "Well," she said to Cornelia, "I don't think there will ever be much chance of ladies traveling in airplanes!"

"I'm not so sure," Cornelia said gently, surprising Samantha with how gracefully she could disagree with Grandmary. "I've read in the newspaper that travel by airplane might be possible one day, even across the ocean."

Samantha looked at Grandmary. She knew Grandmary thought this was nonsense. But her grandmother merely replied, "Perhaps."

Uncle Gard laughed. "By Jupiter, any sort of travel is fine with me! Let them put me in a hot air balloon or in a rickshaw or on an elephant. I'd even let them shoot me out of a cannon!"

"Gardner!" Grandmary exclaimed. She

pretended to be shocked, and Samantha giggled.

"Of course I think the *best* form of travel is sledding," Uncle Gard added. He turned to Samantha. "Don't you, Sam?"

"Oh, yes," Samantha agreed, "only I haven't gone yet this winter."

"Well, why don't we go sledding tomorrow morning?" suggested Cornelia.

"Do you really think . . . ?" Grandmary began.

Cornelia's large brown eyes were soft and earnest. "It's such good, wholesome exercise," she said.

"Please, Grandmary," Samantha pleaded. "I *love* sledding!"

"All right," Grandmary smiled. "Sledding tomorrow morning will be fine."

"Hurrah!" cried Samantha. Right then she made up her mind to give Cornelia something nice for Christmas after all. Maybe bath salts. The kind in the tall bottle with the fancy glass top.

The sun sparkled on Fairwind Hill the next morning. The sky was deep blue and cloudless, the air was clean and cool, and all of Mount Bedford lay below, tucked under a soft thick blanket of snow.

"I love this hill," Uncle Gard said as they pulled the sled to the top. "When I was a boy, I'd come up here to imagine I was in heaven."

Cornelia smiled. "Gard, I think you could imagine *anything* if you tried."

"I couldn't imagine life without you," Gard murmured.

Samantha caught his words. *Uncle Gard is in love!* she said to herself. *He loves Cornelia!*

"Sam," Uncle Gard called over his shoulder, "who's going to steer?"

"You steer the sled, Uncle Gard. I want to be in the middle."

"All right," Uncle Gard laughed. "Let's go!"

The three piled on the sled. Uncle Gard sat in front, then Samantha, and behind them both, Cornelia.

"I feel somewhat like a caboose," Cornelia said, making Samantha laugh.

"Hold on!" Uncle Gard called. With a tremendous whoosh they were gone, skimming down the hillside at top speed.

"Ooooh!" cried Samantha with delight.

"Hurrah for us!" came Cornelia's unladylike shout.

The sled slid faster and faster, skidding and hopping down the hill. "Watch out!" Uncle Gard yelled.

But it was too late.

The sled veered out of control, narrowly missed a tree, and tipped over. The passengers spilled out into the snow.

"Oof!" Samantha grunted, wiping the soft powder from her face.

Uncle Gard was in front of her, laughing and pointing back up the hill. Samantha turned to see what he thought was so funny. It was Cornelia! She had landed on her stomach, and her hat had flown right off her head. She looked most unladylike with her legs tangled, her face red as a beet, and her beautiful hair all stringy and wet. But she was laughing, too! Samantha had never seen anything like it. A grown-up lady who knew how to play.

*The passengers spilled out
into the snow.*

Cornelia is fun! I see why Uncle Gard loves her,
Samantha thought.

"Come on!" Cornelia cried, pulling herself up
and dusting off the snow. "Let's do it again!"

And they did. They sledded until they were so
out of breath, their clothes so wet, and their noses
so red they could do nothing but hurry home to a
hot lunch with Grandmary. After lunch they
decided to go shopping. They piled into Uncle
Gard's automobile, and with a loud "oohwah
oohwah" from the horn, they rumbled off toward
High Street.

This year the stores seemed more beautiful than
ever. Miss Smith's Stationery Shop had a revolving
Christmas tree made of Christmas cards. As a music
box played "Joy to the World," the tree turned
round and round.

Mr. Jerome, the shoemaker, had four
mechanical elves in his window. They hammered,
stitched, and polished tiny shoes. Their mouths

opened and closed as they worked, and
their pointy-hatted heads turned from
side to side.

"Aren't they cute?" Samantha

asked. She had seen the elves every Christmas she could remember, yet each year they delighted her as if she had never seen them before.

"Yes, I love the store windows at Christmas time, too," Cornelia replied.

Next they came to Mr. Carruthers' Candy Shop. Samantha thought Mr. Carruthers' shop was always a wonderful place, but now she thought it was spectacular. Large red bins shaped like sleighs were heaped with sweets.

"Oh, don't those look delicious?" Cornelia pointed to the mounds of light and dark chocolate on a small silver tray inside a glass case. "I just love chocolate truffles," she said.

"Well, these are the finest in Mount Bedford," Mr. Carruthers informed her. "Jolie Chocolates. They arrived just this week from France."

"They do look special," Uncle Gard remarked, "although I prefer jelly beans myself."

Samantha had paused in front of some colored sugar wafers. "Oh, Samantha, wouldn't these be perfect on a gingerbread house?" Cornelia asked her. "When I was a girl, I always decorated a gingerbread house."

"I always decorated a gingerbread house, too,"
Samantha said. "This year Mrs. Hawkins doesn't
have time to help me, though."

"Then why don't you and I make a gingerbread
house?" Cornelia asked. "We could do it tomorrow
morning."

"Oh, I'd like that. I'd like that very much!"
Samantha said. They picked out all the trimmings
right then. Mr. Carruthers filled several paper bags
with lemon drops, sugar wafers, jelly beans, and
honey sticks.

*Cornelia is really too nice for bath
salts,* Samantha thought as they walked
out of the store. *She deserves something
special. Maybe I'll get her handkerchiefs. Linen
handkerchiefs with lace edges.*

When they crossed Felter Street, Samantha
heard the tinkly music of toy pianos. "Let's go to
Schofield's Toy Store!" she cried.

The store was crowded, but Uncle Gard,
Cornelia, and Samantha managed to make their
way inside. Uncle Gard led Cornelia to the back of
the shop to look at the toy soldiers, and Samantha
went straight to the window to look at the dolls.

42

When she saw that the lovely Nutcracker doll was still there, her heart sank. She'd hoped it would be gone because Grandmary had bought it for her, but she knew that was a foolish hope. Grandmary didn't even know that Samantha wanted this doll more than anything in the world. Grandmary *couldn't* know that because Samantha hadn't told her. And now Samantha was sure that someone else would buy the doll for some other girl—maybe for one of the girls in the store right this minute.

Just then a hand reached into the display and picked up the beautiful Nutcracker doll. "Oh, look at this doll! Isn't she exquisite?"

Samantha was startled. She hadn't heard anyone come up behind her. She turned to find Cornelia.

"And look at the tiny Nutcracker in her arms," Cornelia exclaimed. "This is the most wonderful doll in the store. Don't you think so, Samantha?"

"Oh, yes," Samantha agreed out loud. To herself she said, *Cornelia understands. She knows what's special.* And for just a moment, she forgot to be sad about the doll she would never have.

Just then Uncle Gard returned. "The toy

soldiers said we'd better march. Grandmary will worry if we're late."

They pushed their way out of the busy store, but when they reached the car Samantha announced, "I won't be coming home with you."

"What do you mean?" Uncle Gard asked.

"I—I forgot something. I forgot to—to buy the vanilla Mrs. Hawkins asked me to pick up for her," Samantha lied. "I'll get it and walk home."

"Nonsense, Sam," Uncle Gard said. "We'll go together."

"No—no, really," Samantha said, "I would rather go alone and walk. I love the streets at Christmas time."

Uncle Gard was about to say no again, but something in Samantha's voice must have told him this was important. After a pause he said, "All right, Sam, go if you want. But don't be late!"

When she was sure the automobile had turned the corner, Samantha ran back up High Street to Mr. Carruthers' Candy Shop. The little bell over the door tinkled as she went inside. "Well, young lady," Mr. Carruthers said, "how can I help you this time?"

"A pound of Jolie French chocolates, please."

"A whole pound?" Mr. Carruthers asked, his white eyebrows twitching up with surprise.

"A whole pound," Samantha repeated.

"This must be for someone really special, Samantha."

"Oh, yes, Mr. Carruthers—someone *very* special."

EXCHANGING GIFTS

 On Christmas Eve morning, Samantha and Cornelia put the finishing touches on their gingerbread house. Their hands were sticky with icing and Samantha's cheek was striped with chocolate, but their gingerbread cottage was neat and tidy. It wasn't as large as the house Samantha had planned, and it didn't have a drawbridge, but there was a path of colored sugar wafers that looked like cobblestones leading up to the front door.

"You're clever in the kitchen, Miss Cornelia," Mrs. Hawkins said.

Cornelia blushed and pushed a silky curl out of her eyes. "Oh, it's nothing really," she answered.

"I've always enjoyed cooking, Mrs. Hawkins."

"Well, it's a credit to you," Mrs. Hawkins declared solemnly. "Many a lady nowadays wouldn't know batter from butter!"

"Did I hear someone say 'butter'?" Uncle Gard asked, coming into the kitchen. "Good grief, Mrs. Hawkins! I do hope you're not buttering up Cornelia. We wouldn't want her to slip away!"

Samantha groaned. "Uncle Gard, that's an awful joke."

"Is it?" Uncle Gard asked innocently. "Well, I suppose it's an awful *good* joke."

"Oh, Uncle Gard, please stop," Samantha said.

"Okay, Sam. But it's time to go if we want to find our Christmas tree. Hawkins has already harnessed the horses."

"I'll be ready before you can say 'Merry Christmas'!" Samantha called, racing to get her mittens, hat, and coat.

Hawkins held the horses steady as Samantha and Uncle Gard climbed into the sleigh. Uncle Gard slapped the reins hard over the horses' backs, and  the sleigh glided down the path to the street. For several minutes Samantha and her uncle rode in silence. They shared the red wool blanket and waved to passing neighbors. Then, almost to herself, Samantha said, "Tomorrow is Christmas."

"It's come pretty quickly, hasn't it, Sam?"

"No, I don't think so," Samantha replied. "I've been planning for months. And of course," she added with a mischievous smile, "it took a long time to get *your* present ready."

"Oh?" Uncle Gard asked, pretending not to be interested.

"Yes. It's the nicest present of all, and you'll

never, never guess what it is," Samantha said.

"Of course I will!" Uncle Gard announced. "Let me try. Is it smaller than a breadbox?"

"Quite a bit, yes."

"Is it green?"

"Parts of it are," Samantha told him.

"Could I ride on it?"

"Not at all," Samantha giggled.

"Does it sing?"

"No."

"Can it do handsprings?"

Samantha laughed. "No! Guess some more."

"Is it something that closes up?"

"It could . . ." Samantha said cautiously.

"Could I wear it on my head in summer?"

"You'd look silly if you did!"

"Aha! I know what it is!" Uncle Gard declared.

"Tell me," Samantha said.

"It's a baby turtle, of course."

"A baby turtle?" Samantha gasped. "How do you figure that, Uncle Gard?"

"Because, Sam, everyone knows a baby turtle is smaller than a breadbox, cannot sing or do handsprings, is part green, can close up, cannot be

ridden, and would look silly on my head in
summer."

"Well, you're wrong," Samantha said. "It's not
a baby turtle. It's something I made. And it's very
beautiful. In fact, it is the most beautiful thing I've
ever made for anyone."

"I'm sure I will love it, Sam," Uncle Gard said.

"I wonder what you'll give *me* for Christmas?"
Samantha asked slyly.

"No, you don't!" Uncle Gard said. "Don't you
try to trick me into telling you."

"Just give me some clues. Please, Uncle Gard,"
Samantha begged.

"Okay, I'll give you three clues and no more.
Clue number one: like a good schoolgirl, it uses
notes. Clue number two: unlike Samantha, it always
plays alone. Clue number three: it's *bound* to please
you."

Samantha was so puzzled by these clues that
she sat deep in thought while the sleigh glided
through the silent woods. When they reached the
frozen river, Uncle Gard stopped the horses and
tied the reins to a low willow branch. He lifted an
axe from the back of the sleigh and caught

Samantha's hand as she jumped down into the soft snow. Then they walked together, looking for just the right tree.

"This is it, Uncle Gard," Samantha said at last.

"You're right, Samantha. It's a real beauty."

Uncle Gard chopped away. The axe's loud whacks echoed through the stillness, and Samantha didn't talk as they dragged the tree back to the sleigh. On the way home, the horses' bells jingled brightly to the clip-clop rhythm of their hooves.

"I believe Mrs. Hawkins really outdid herself this year," Uncle Gard said as he pushed his chair back from the table. "Dinner was a feast!"

The aroma of plum pudding still hung in the air. Red candles burned low in their polished holders. And Samantha couldn't wait a moment longer. "Grandmary, now may we decorate the tree?" she asked.

"Of course," Grandmary replied.

They gathered in the parlor and began to

unpack the ornaments. Grandmary lifted a pair of
little glass slippers out of the big oak chest. "These
belong where they'll catch the light," she said. "I've
watched them sparkle since I was six
years old." She draped their golden
cord over a long branch. Uncle Gard
put a brass trumpet nearby. Cornelia
placed the long-necked crystal swans near the top
of the tree, where they seemed to float in the
branches. And Samantha hung all of her blue silk
angels right in the front, where Cornelia insisted
they should be.

Soon it was time to attach the little white
candles. Then slowly, one by one, Uncle Gard lit
them. The effect was glorious. China rosebuds
gleamed, crystal swans sparkled, and silk angels
shone in the flickering light. Foil-wrapped sugar
plums bobbed and twinkled, and miniature brass
trumpets winked brightly. Grandmary's glass
slippers seemed to dance.

They watched in silence, until Cornelia stepped
over to the piano and began to play and sing:

"O Christmas tree, O Christmas tree,
How lovely are your branches."

Uncle Gard joined in, and Samantha and Grandmary sang, too. When the song was finished,
Cornelia began another Christmas carol. They all
sang and sang until the last candles on their
beautiful tree burned low.

Later that night, while Samantha lay awake
listening to street carolers in the distance, she
thought again of the lovely Nutcracker doll. *Right
now she's probably under some girl's Christmas tree,
wrapped in pretty paper and waiting to be opened,*
Samantha thought. She tried to think of something
else, but it was no use. *If only I had even asked*

"Not at all, dear, I'm quite perplexed so far."

Very slowly Grandmary took off the paper. When she found the heart-shaped sachet she said, "Samantha, you're a dear and clever girl. This is very lovely."

Next came a present from Uncle Gard to Samantha. "Here's your answer to those riddles, Sam," he said.

Samantha ripped off the wrapping paper and found a red leather book of Christmas carols. She turned the pages carefully, humming songs as she  went. When she reached the end of the book, Samantha found a golden key. She wound it and a music box began to play her favorite song of all—"O Christmas Tree."

"Now I understand, Uncle Gard!" Samantha exclaimed. "You said my present would use notes and play alone because it's a music box. And it *is* bound to please me because it's a book of my favorite Christmas carols, too. Now I can listen to them all year round. Thank you."

Samantha was about to give Uncle Gard a small square box covered in blue tissue paper, but

Cornelia handed her a large package instead.

"Go ahead, open yours first, Sam," Uncle Gard said with a wink.

Samantha had never seen anything wrapped so elegantly. She untied the silk ribbon and carefully rolled it up. "Cornelia, is this from New York?" asked Samantha.

"Open it and see."

Samantha smoothed away the silvery wrapping paper and slowly lifted the lid from the box. "Cornelia!" she gasped. "It's the Nutcracker doll! Oh, I've wanted this doll for the longest time. How did you ever know?"

"I didn't know, Samantha," Cornelia said. "Truly I didn't. It's only that *I* liked the doll so much I thought perhaps you might, too."

"I do," Samantha said. She hugged the doll as if she'd never let it go. "I love her. I love her more than any other doll in the whole world. Thank you, Cornelia. Thank you so much!"

With the doll still in her arms, Samantha reached under the tree. Once again she picked up the small square box wrapped in blue tissue paper.

Samantha hugged the doll
as if she'd never let it go.

But this time she turned to Cornelia and handed it to her. "Merry Christmas, Cornelia," Samantha whispered, suddenly shy.

"And Merry Christmas, Uncle Gard," Samantha said more loudly, handing him a larger package tied with a big pink bow.

Uncle Gard got his present unwrapped first. "By Jove, Sam!" he said when he opened the candy. "There must be a pound of chocolates here. You do spoil me!"

"Oh, Samantha, it's so very pretty!" Cornelia exclaimed when she saw the decorated box. "Why, look at all these tiny pictures! This must have taken you a long time to make."

"It did," Samantha said honestly. "That box took me longer than any other thing I've made. Ever!"

"I will keep my jewelry in it and treasure it always," Cornelia said.

Samantha caught Uncle Gard's happy wink. She thought he guessed that the box had been made for cuff links, but he seemed to understand why she'd given it to Cornelia.

Now Uncle Gard turned to Cornelia and said,

"I think you need something special to keep in such a beautiful box, my dear." He handed her a tiny gift wrapped in dark red paper with a large gold bow on top. When Cornelia opened it, a diamond ring sparkled in the Christmas morning sunlight.

"Oh, Gard," she murmured softly.

But Samantha was so overjoyed she shouted, "It's an engagement ring! They're going to marry! Grandmary, isn't it wonderful?"

"Children, I'm so happy." Grandmary's voice was quivery, and she had to dab her eyes with her hankie.

"When is the wedding?" Samantha couldn't wait to find out.

"In March," the couple answered together.

"You *will* be my bridesmaid, won't you, Samantha?" Cornelia asked.

"Yes, I'd love to!" Samantha answered, and gave her a big hug. "Cornelia, this *has* been the best Christmas ever!!!"

LOOKING BACK 1904

A Peek Into the Past

An elaborate turn-of-the-century Christmas celebration

To Samantha, Christmas meant sleigh bells, jolly
Saint Nick, carolers, decorations everywhere, and
piles of presents under the tree. Samantha's turn-of-
the-century Christmas was the biggest,
grandest, and happiest celebration of the
year. Wealthy people like Grandmary
were proud of their houses and their
possessions. Christmas was the perfect time to show them off with
elaborate decorations and extrava-
gant parties. It was fashionable to
make Christmas the most glorious

62

Jolly Saint Nick

holiday of the year.

By 1904, fine steamships carried rich Americans on vacation trips to Europe. Americans who traveled abroad were fascinated with the lives of people in England—especially kings, queens, princes, and princesses. Many Americans began to imitate wealthy people in England. They sent Christmas cards like the English did. They also made the Christmas tree the dazzling centerpiece of the holiday.

Christmas
card, 1904

Christmas trees began as a German tradition, but elaborately decorated trees were especially popular in England because of Queen Victoria. She had the first

A family gathers at Christmas

Children from well-to-do families received many gifts.

one in Windsor Castle decorated for her nine children. Many Americans followed the English tradition of hanging small gifts like watches, tops, and paint boxes from their trees. Exquisite glass ornaments were imported from Germany.

Just like today, some Christmas trees were decorated with paper chains, strings of popcorn and cranberries, and cookies cut in different shapes. But trees were lighted with candles rather than with electric lights, and someone had to stand by with water and a sponge because fires started very easily. Still, people thought it was worth the effort when they saw a tree with all of its candles lit, looking as if stars had settled on every branch.

And under the tree? In households like Grandmary's there were presents to make any child's dreams come true. Since ships could cross the ocean quickly and safely, many presents were imported from Europe. For children there were books from England, dolls from Germany, music boxes from Switzerland, and chocolates from France. But one popular toy in Samantha's time was very American. It was a cheery-looking bear called a Teddy Bear, named after the President of the United States, Theodore "Teddy" Roosevelt.

Christmas morning

Christmas stockings were filled with smaller gifts like pens, hair ribbons, and candies. Children like Samantha were showered with treats and gifts. Christmas was a good time to be a child in a household like Grandmary's.

Teddy Bears, a popular present in 1904

Big family gatherings were fashionable, and on Christmas Day Americans

The table set for an elegant Christmas feast

got together with all their relatives and family friends for an elaborate dinner. In 1904, people didn't worry about their figures the way we do now. In fact, it was considered a sign of success to be plump. So Christmas dinner was an enormous feast with soup, fish, ham, and a golden-brown goose. There were many different kinds of breads, creamed vegetables, and mounds of potatoes drenched in gravy. To top it all off, there was a steaming plum pudding decorated

with a sprig of holly, another tradition the Americans copied from the English. After dinner there would be singing, games of charades, pantomimes, and

Plum pudding

puppet shows for the children.

Of course, Christmas wasn't a holiday for everyone. For servants like Mr. and Mrs. Hawkins and Elsa, Christmas meant more work than usual. There was a lot of cooking, cleaning, and laundry to do to get ready for the holiday. Some American households followed another English tradition of giving servants a day off after Christmas. December 26 was called *Boxing Day* because servants got their presents, or Christmas boxes, then. Often women like Grandmary brought gifts of food and clothes to orphanages and hospitals on that day, too. They thought it was important to share a Christmas in which they had so much with people who had less.

If the postcard has already
been removed from this book
and you would like to receive
a Pleasant Company catalogue,
please send your full name
and address to:

PLEASANT COMPANY
P.O. Box 620497
Middleton, WI 53562-9940
or, call our toll-free number
1-800-845-0005